SP...
POEMS

SPOOKY POEMS

ADRIAN HENRI

ILLUSTRATED BY
WENDY SMITH

BLOOMSBURY
CHILDREN'S
BOOKS

First published in Great Britain in 2001
Bloomsbury Publishing Plc, 38 Soho Square, London, W1D 3HB

Text copyright © Adrian Henri 2001
Illustrations copyright © Wendy Smith 2001

The moral right of the author has been asserted
A CIP catalogue record of this book is available from the
British Library

ISBN 0 7475 4422 0

Printed in England by Clays Ltd, St Ives plc

10 9 8 7 6 5 4 3 2 1

Contents

Skeleton Song

there's no room
in the catacombs
no more room
in the friendly gloom
we're happy in the catacombs
here inside our cosy tombs
no more trouble
no more fuss
don't come here
disturbing us
take your bones
to a grave of your own
and leave us skeletons
alone

In the Empty Classroom

Six o'clock in the empty classroom,
and the clock has just been put back an hour
for the end of summertime. Shadows
edge between the desks, lose themselves
in the blackboard's inky depths.
The smell of disinfectant sulks uneasily
in corners, resents the encroaching mustiness.

Suddenly,
the lights come on. Harsh yellow
blacks out the windows. Then,
off again. Dazzled walls
can just make out the neon glow
of the T.V. The blue, buzzing screen
mutters words in no known language.
On, off again. Shadows, darkness, silence.
The faint shuffle of the caretaker's feet,
carefully avoiding this corridor.

Distant chimes of midnight,
the sound of last buses.
From up the stairs, the halting,
haunting sound of a piano
echoes through the building. Waltzes,
    mazurkas,
stumble over their notes, repeat their
    corrections,
reluctantly, die away
at the first sign of day.

Pigeons stalk the playground.

The yawning gate
awaits the tread of morning feet.

Winter Moon

Orange sunset low across the woods
The shock of cold as you breathe in
daylight gone, the night begins
All too soon the winter moon

Moorhens chatter on the icy lake
A dog patters across crisp grass
Shadows lurk across the path
All too soon the winter moon

Families of mice and voles
Huddle safe inside their holes
Marmalade light yields to the night
All too soon the winter moon

Trees clasp hands, branches dance
Silent spectral mists advance
Distant echoes of a waltz
All too soon the winter moon

Holly and bramble tear your clothes
Someone sleeps with the briar rose
Dark shapes cluster, shadows loom
All too soon the winter moon

Tawny owls wake and shiver
Something makes the branches quiver
Flits across the rising gloom

All too soon the winter moon

Ghost Story

Half an hour to closing time:
in the Library basement
the phantom Lady in Red
flits from bookcase to bookcase
shys from the cries
of excited Brownies
trying to win their Ghosthunter badges.

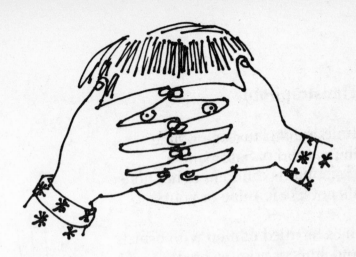

The Face

What is the face that comes at midnight?
What is the sound that won't go away?

What is the face that's there at morning?
What is the sound I hear when I play?

What is the face I see at lunchtime?
What is the sound when the wind blows chill?

What is the face beyond the lamplight?
What is the sound that lingers still?

This is the face that I remember
That is the sound I can't forget
This is the sound I've never heard
That is the face I've never met.

Claustrophobia

Emily's got claustrophobia
She's afraid of Santa Claus
Christmas is different in her house
It's not like in mine or yours

She's terrified of men with beards
And suits of brightest red
Sneaking down the chimney
While she's fast asleep in bed

She's hidden away her stockings
At the back of the chest of drawers
She's covered up the fireplace
And locked the bedroom door

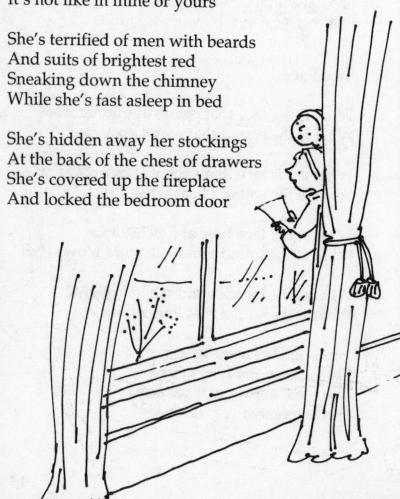

A kiss from Father Christmas
Is the thing she dreads the most
She'd rather be hugged by Dracula
or Jacob Marley's ghost

She hates holly, robins and ivy
She won't go and play in the snow
You'll never catch her standing
Beneath the mistletoe

Emily's got claustrophobia
Carol singers make her feel queer
Don't wish her a Merry Christmas
She's hiding away till New Year.

The Gorby

They're laughing at my silly face
silliest of all the human race
They're laughing at my silly dance
clumsier than an elephant's
They're laughing at my staring eyes
They're laughing at my giant size
'Look at the Gorby' 'What a Clown'
They shout as they run off into town.

But wait until the sun has set
they'll learn a game they won't forget
A movement in the shadows, then,
one of them won't be seen again.

Is it beetroot stains my fingers?
Or blackberry-juice that makes them red?
What is this dark stain that lingers?
What makes them think they're safe in bed?

He who laughs last his
laughter's stronger
When *the* Gorby laughs
his laugh lasts longer.

Necronomicon

Look in the Book of Dead Names,
run your eyes down the list,
the missing and the missed.
Open the worm-eaten cover,
yellow musty pages. The smell
of countless ages. The Book of Eibon.
Read on. Names you heard
in your dream, the grinding
of the wheel. Chthulu, Yog-Sothoth,
Lloigor, Al-Alhazred,
Dagon, Hastur, Azathoth,
all the long undead. Pause.
Turn the last page.
A familiar name . . .

         . . . yours.

Blood Brothers

Jim Dracula and Albert Frankenstein
live on a council estate near Crewe.
The two work on the night shift,
and often travel in together on the bus.
Jim carries his blood sandwiches
in a blue plastic lunchbox, and Albert
always has a flask of steaming, bright green liquid.
Jim runs a one-man transfusion service;
Albert works on the assembly-line
in a body factory.

'I've always been clever with my hands,'
says Albert
'It's a matter of taste, I suppose,'
says Jim,
licking his lips.

Jim Dracula and Albert Frankenstein
like to roam but are happiest at home
with their work, and can't wait to get back.
Jim has packed his wooden stake and bit of
    Cheshire soil
in a brand new vinyl coffin,
ready for his package-tour of Transylvania.

Albert has dozed off
while reading his manual of spare-part surgery
in a laboratory high in the mountains.

Jim Dracula and Albert Frankenstein
will be back to the old routine next week,
off to work as the sun sets,
and tucked up in the vault by breakfast-time;
down to the graveyard for fresh supplies;
or fluttering up the front of tower-blocks.

'I haven't had a bite all day,'
says Jim
'Give us a hand,'
says Albert,
'This one's got one foot
in the grave.'

The Green Light

There's a green light in at the window
There's a green light shining on the stair
There's a sound where the green light comes
    from
But I can't see anything there.

There's a green light shining from the
    doorway
There's a green light glows in the night
There's a shape where the green light comes
    from
And it's not a pretty sight.

There's a green light growing clearer
There's a green light like the sea
There's a *something* getting nearer
And I think it's after me.

There's a green light all around me
There's a green light fills the skies
There's a green light that surrounds me
And it's looking in my eyes . . .

The Phantom Lollipop Lady

The phantom lollipop lady
haunts the crossroads
where the old school used to be;
they closed it down in 1973.

The old lollipop lady
loved her job, and stood there
for seven years altogether,
no matter how bad the weather.

When they pulled the old school down
she still stood there every day:
a pocketful of sweets for the little ones,
smiles and a joke for the big ones.

One day the lollipop lady
was taken away to hospital.
Without her standing there
the corner looked, somehow, bare.

After a month and two operations
the lollipop lady died;
the children felt something missing:
she had made her final crossing.

Now if you go down alone at dusk
just before the streetlights go on,
look closely at the corner over there:
in the shadows by the lamp-post you'll see her.

Helping phantom children across the street,
holding up the traffic with a ghostly hand;
at the twilight crossing where four roads meet
the phantom lollipop lady stands.

Queen Tut

Fancy
a mummy
all shut up
in a great big case
with a nasty face;
when you see them
in a museum
it's fine:
but I'm glad she's
Tutankhamun
's mum,
not mine.

Sticks and Stones

Why do they cry over a book
or things they've heard? They
don't hurt, they're only words;
it's just absurd.

I can't see why, when I'm scared
of the telly, they tell me 'It's not real',
when old films make them feel
all weepy. It's creepy.

They don't have to look.
They could close the book.
It's not like being lost in the park,
or left alone in the dark.

That's why
I cry.

The Lurkers

On our Estate
When it's getting late
In the middle of the night
They come in flocks
From beneath tower-blocks
And crawl towards the light

Down the Crescent
Up the Drive
Late at night
They come alive
Lurking here and lurking there
Sniffing at the midnight air

Up the Shopping Centre
You might just hear their call
Something like a bin-bag
Moving by the wall

Lurking at the bus-stop
Seen through broken glass
Something dark and slimy
Down the underpass

On our Estate
When it's getting late
In the middle of the night
There are things that lurk
About their work
Till dawn puts them to flight.

I Saw

I'm *sure*
I saw a dinosaur
just across the road,
peeping out above Tesco
and the DIY store.
I did,
just before:
there's an enormous foot-mark
on the car park
and a Ford Escort
squashed flat; apart from that
there's an awful mess
where it looks like something's tripped
over a skip.

There was
that awful sound, too,
just like thunder, or the noise
the bin-lorries make
when they chew up the rubbish.

Perhaps I should go and investigate.

On second thoughts,
I think I'll just wait.

Nightmare Cemetery

Don't go down with me today
to Nightmare Cemetery
You don't know what you'll see today
in Nightmare Cemetery

Don't go through the gates today
to Nightmare Cemetery
You don't know what waits today
in Nightmare Cemetery

Don't go down the lane today
to Nightmare Cemetery
There you might remain today
in Nightmare Cemetery

Don't go down the road today
to Nightmare Cemetery
Haunt of bat and toad today
in Nightmare Cemetery

The sun will never shine today
in Nightmare Cemetery
Horrors wait in line today
in Nightmare Cemetery

Close the gates and step inside
Much too late to try and hide
Hear the hinges creak with glee
I'll be waiting, just you see,
You're here for ever, just like me
in Nightmare Cemetery.

This poem is not . . .

This poem is not a wolf.

It lives in the depths of forests.
It lurks in the dark where you can't see it.
It hunts in a pack with other poems.
It has big shiny teeth.
It has eyes that glow red in the dark.

This poem is not a wolf.

You won't find it in a zoo,
though you might find it dressed in sheep's
    clothing
or even disguised as your grandmother.

This poem is not a wolf.

Who's afraid of the big bad poem,
big bad poem, big bad poem?
Who's afraid . . .
. . . who?

The Dark

I don't like the dark coming down on my
head
It feels like a blanket thrown over the bed
I don't like the dark coming down on my
head

I don't like the dark coming down over me
It feels like the room's full of things I can't see
I don't like the dark coming down over me

There isn't enough light from under the door
It only just reaches the edge of the floor
There isn't enough light from under the door

I wish that my dad hadn't put out the light
It feels like there's something that's just out of
sight
I wish that my dad hadn't put out the light

But under the bedclothes it's warm and secure
You can't see the ceiling you can't see the floor
Yes, under the bedclothes it's warm and secure
So I think I'll stay here till it's daylight once
more.

The Haunted Disco

When it's half-past three in the morning
right through to break of day,
a phantom DJ opens up
for the dead to come and play.

The coloured lights are flashing,
and the crowd are on their feet,
but there's no sound of them dancing
to the ghostly disco-beat.

When there's ice between your shoulders,
and the hairs rise on your neck,
and you don't know who you're dancing with
at the haunted discotheque.

When you daren't look at your partner,
and you fear their bony hand,
the go-go ghosts all boogie
to an ancient, nameless band.

The graveyard sounds are all around
the mist drifts everywhere,
but the ghastly crowds in mini-shrouds
rave on without a care.

When there's ice between your shoulders,
and the hairs rise on your neck,
and you know you'll dance for ever
in the haunted discotheque.

Gallowgates

Gallowgates at midnight
silence on the stairs
never let the shadows
catch you unawares

Gallowgates at midnight
hear the churchyard chime
knowing that the last stroke
tells you it's time

Gallowgates at midnight
close your eyes and pray
hoping that the darkness
fades before the day

Gallowgates at midnight
something at the gate
too late now for moonlight
turn and meet your fate.

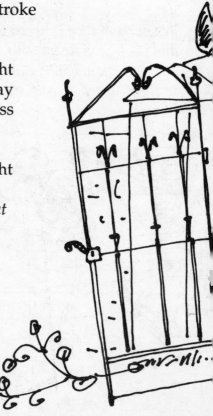

There is someone in my house . . .

There is someone in my house.

The step is in pieces and a bookshelf has fallen off
the wall. All night. there are hushed sounds
almost drowned in city traffic.

There is someone in my house.

A picture fell yesterday and a window has cracked
mysteriously. Doors slam. The towel
is never where I left it.

There is someone in my house.

The walls whisper. The floorboards creak
to themselves. The telephone will not speak
unless it is spoken to. Who
is there? Why
do I never see you?

There is someone in my house . . .

Moon Clover

Black-hearted clover
away from our sight
Why do you blossom
only at night?

Why do you bloom
as the moon fills the sky?
Why do you flourish
away from our eyes?

Black-hearted moon-clover
shunning the day
Remember the field
Where we walked yesterday.

The Stiperstones
A Shropshire tale

Don't go walking in the mountains
Don't go near the Stiperstones
See the hedge of blackened hawthorn
Writhe and twist like ancient bones

Once you leave the road to Stretton
Past the ruined carding-mill
Lurks a mist that summer sunlight
Can't disperse: it lingers still

Darkened is the road to Wenlock
Shadowed is the road to Clee
Darker shapes that cluster nearer
Stiperstones are calling me

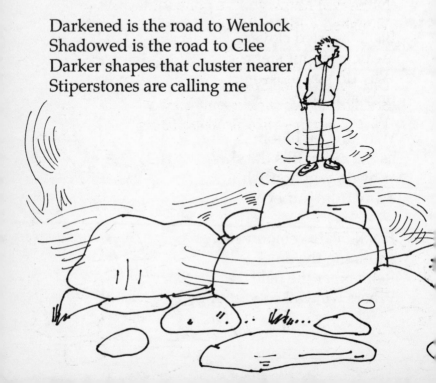

Feel the fog cling ever closer
Feel the path rise steeper still
Feel the twisted hedge surround you
At the summit of the hill

Huge the rocks rise on the skyline
Loud the wind roars in your ears
Stiperstones are calling, calling
Down the echoes of the years

Lie down and forget your sorrow
Let your troubles flow away
None will know you've gone tomorrow
Vanished with the break of day

Don't go walking in the mountains
Don't go near the Stiperstones
See the hedge of ancient hawthorn
Writhe and twist like blackened bones

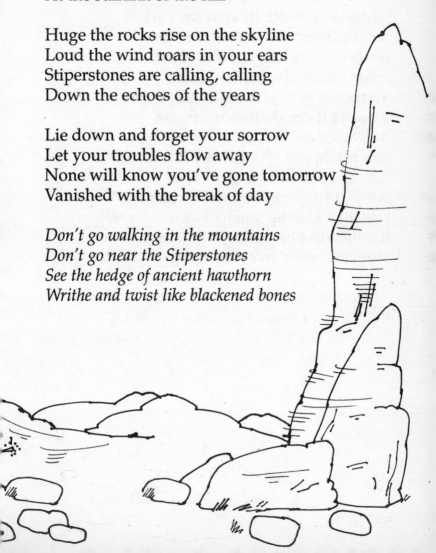

Jenny Greenteeth

A Legend of Sefton Park

Jenny Greenteeth lives in the Park,
waits for the children after dark,
watches them busy at their play,
waits for the day to fade away,
till there's no one there to see or hear
if one of them should disappear.

You might just glimpse her if you take
the shady path beside the lake;
but if it's getting late don't linger, or
you may feel the touch of a clammy finger.
If you're in The Dell and you hear a sound
hurry on and don't turn round.

In the silence by the rusting gates
the shade of Jenny Greenteeth waits.

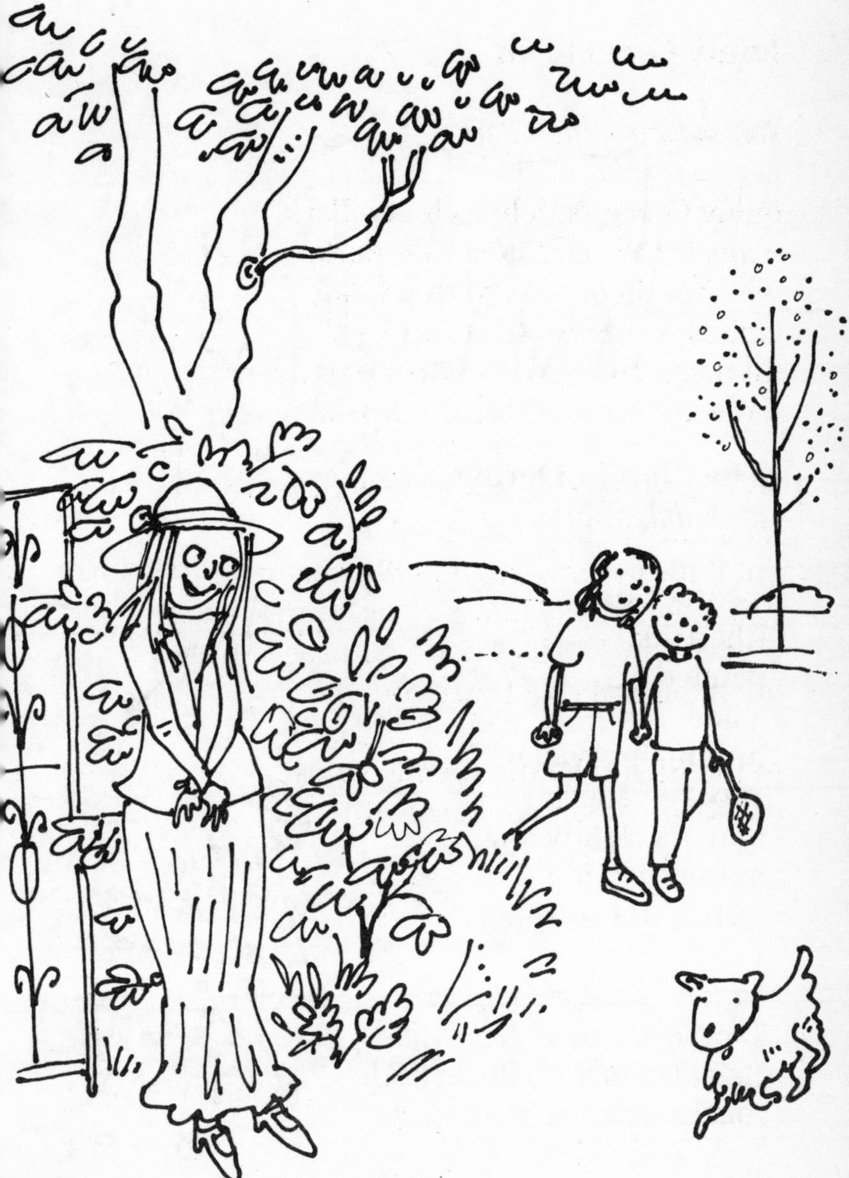

The Lion in Derbyshire
for Frank Milner

George Stubbs
(the artist)
painted
a lion
lurking in a valley,
a rocky valley,
under a cloudy sky
in Derbyshire.
A lion, in Derbyshire!

He's the Beast of Bolsover
The Nightmare of New Mills
He's the Curse of Chesterfield
And he stalks the Derby hills

George Stubbs
(the artist)
painted
a white horse
going about its horsey business
in a dark valley,
when suddenly
a fierce, hot smell;
gruff sounds drown the birdsong,
the wind across the crags:
a lion!
A lion, in Derbyshire!

He's the Curse of Chesterfield
The Nightmare of New Mills
He's the Beast of Bolsover
And he stalks the Derby Hills

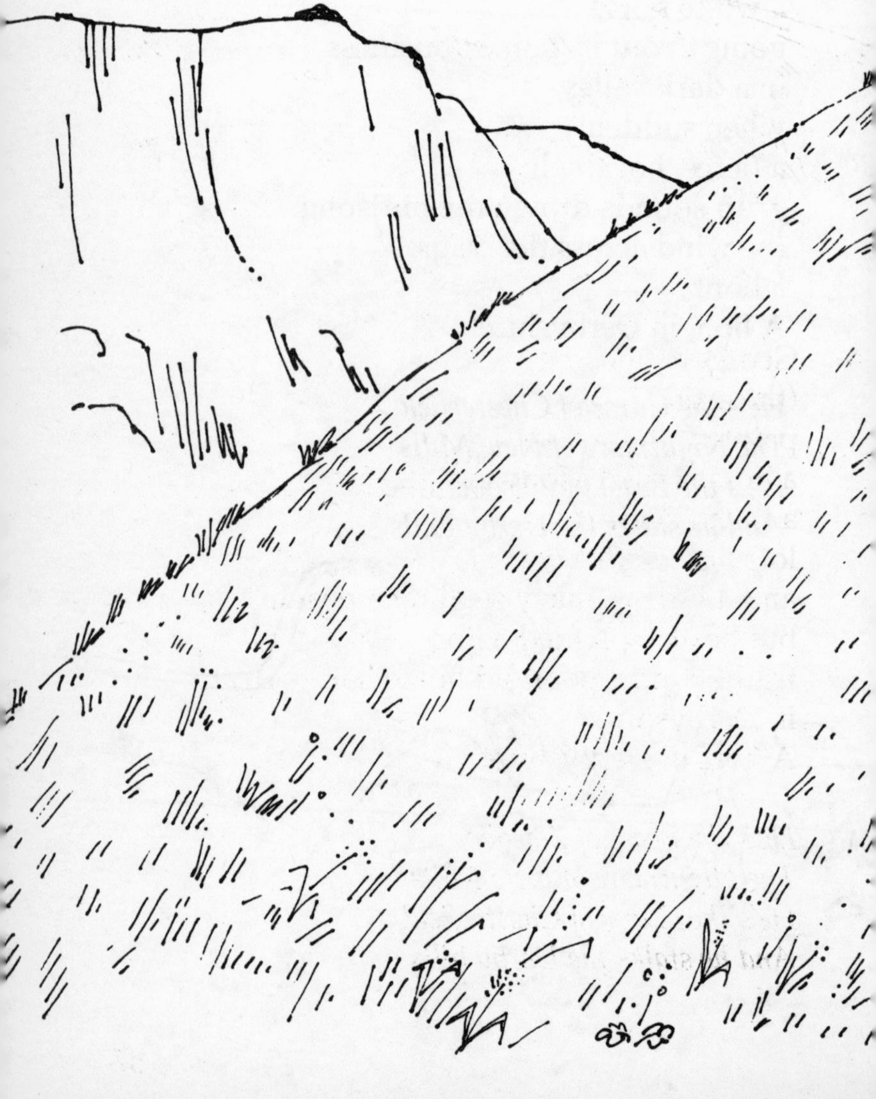

George Stubbs
(the artist)
painted
a horse called Molly Longlegs,
a Lincolnshire ox,
lots of famous people,
and a little monkey stealing a peach:
but he also painted a lion
frightening a poor old horse half to death
in Derbyshire.
A lion, in Derbyshire!

He's the Beast of Bolsover
The Nightmare of New Mills
He's the Curse of Chesterfield
And he stalks the Derby hills

Pink Lady

There's a ghost that's sometimes seen
outside Room 14. She's always dressed
in pink. Some girls think
she looks just like the old Head, Mrs Green.
Rosa, the Italian cleaner, has certainly
seen her. She ran downstairs
white with fear, shouting 'Mama Mia!'
They say she waits outside the door
just after four. I wonder
who she's waiting for . . .?

The Heart Poem

the hands of the clock move
minute
by minute   by minute   by minute

the digits shift
second
by second   by second   by second

arteries slow
minute
by minute   by minute   by minute

veins stiffen
second
by second   by second   by second

the last tube-train
pulls into the platform
minute
by minute   by minute   by minute

a barge clogged with weeds
on the silted canal
second
by second   by second   by second

the line on the graph paper
slowly straightens
minute
by minute   by minute   by minute

the small green dot on the screen
slowly fading
second
by second   by second   by second

one last
minute   minute   minute
one last
second   second   second
before
the
silence   silence   silence